Alice's World Record

Written by

Tim Kennemore

Illustrated by

Mike Spoor

EERDMANS BOOKS FOR YOUNG READERS
GRAND RAPIDS, MICHIGAN / CAMBRIDGE, U.K.

First published in 2006
by Andersen Press, Ltd,
20 Vauxhall Bridge Road
London SW1V 2SA England

This edition published 2008 by
Eerdmans Books for Young Readers,
an imprint of Wm. B. Eerdmans Publishing Co.

Wm. B. Eerdmans Publishing Co.
2140 Oak Industrial Dr. N.E., Grand Rapids, Michigan 49505
P.O. Box 163, Cambridge CB3 9PU U.K.
www.eerdmans.com/youngreaders

Printed in the United States of America

08 09 10 11 12   8 7 6 5 4 3 2 1

Library of Congress Cataloging-in-Publication Data

Kennemore, Tim.
Alice's world record / by Tim Kennemore; illustrated by Mike Spoor.
p.   cm.

Summary: On the way to their grandparents' house, Alice beats her older brother
Oliver at the alphabet game for the first time ever, making him so miserable that
he reacts in a way that changes him and his status as favorite grandchild.

ISBN 978-0-8028-5336-3 (alk. paper)

[1. Winning and losing — Fiction. 2. Family life — Fiction. 3. Brothers
and sisters — Fiction. 4. Grandparents — Fiction. 5. Chess — Fiction.]
I. Spoor, Mike, ill. II. Title.
PZ7.K392Alm 2008
[E] — dc22
2008001736

Text type set in Lexicon

Contents

1. Polly Penguin Done It   1

2. Rainbow Dice   6

3. You Win Three Bananas   11

4. Pavement Narrows Quarter-mile Ahead   21

5. Grandma and Grandpa Fox   35

6. Top of the World   48

7. Recently Buried Chickens   58

8. Checkmate   66

9. P-Q   71

1

Polly Penguin Done It

One Monday, as Alice Singer's family was sitting down to dinner, there came the most dreadful noise from the front room.

The noise sounded like this:

"OHNOEEEAARRGGH!ARGLE!YARG!WHE RE'SROSIEI'MGONNAKILLHERSCLURBLEAAR GHYURGGHHH!"

It was the sound of Alice's brother Oliver losing his temper.

Everyone looked at Alice's little sister Rosie.

"Polly Penguin done it," said Rosie.

Oliver stormed into the kitchen waving what looked like a rather large peanut butter and jelly sandwich.

"Look what she's done!" he shouted.

Everyone looked.

"She's spread strawberry jelly all over my school library book! All over *Chess Openings for Improving Players, Part One!*"

"Polly Penguin done it," said Rosie, sadly. Rosie was too young and too terrible to have a real pet of her own. Instead she had Polly Penguin. Polly Penguin, who had once been Alice's favorite stuffed animal, lived in a shoebox out on the patio with Alice's guinea pig Aminal and Oliver's rabbit Peter.

Whenever Rosie was caught doing something naughty, she would say, "Polly Penguin done it."

The damage done by Polly Penguin to the Singers' house was almost unbelievable for one small stuffed animal. Polly Penguin's favorite game was to unwind a whole roll of toilet paper from the cardboard and wrap it all around the house. Polly Penguin liked to put people's shoes in the washing machine with a bar of soap and then turn it on. Only last week Polly Penguin had been so very, very bad as to take a large frozen chicken, which was thawing in the kitchen, and

to bury it in a hole in the backyard. There had been a lot of trouble over that.

And now this.

"Look what you've done!" screamed Oliver. "I'll get into trouble, and it's the Chess Tournament tomorrow, and it's the most important day of my life! I hate you! I don't want you for my sister! I want to go and live with Grandma Fox in Bristol!"

Grandma Fox was Mom's mom. She was Oliver's favorite grandparent, and he was her favorite grandchild. They both believed in doing things properly, keeping things tidy, and making sure that small, naughty children were looked after by other people and kept well out of their way, preferably locked up securely in a cage.

"Polly Penguin done it," said Rosie patiently.

Mom said that as Rosie wasn't looking after Polly Penguin properly, from now on Rosie would be punished for all the things Polly Penguin did wrong.

Rosie looked at Oliver's strawberry chess book, thought about things for a while, and said: "Alice done it!"

"Alice *did* it!" said Oliver, who was very upset, but not so upset that he was going to let Rosie get away with saying things the wrong way.

"I didn't do it!" shouted Alice.

"I don't mean that you *did* it," said Oliver, going pink in the face with anger and with trying to explain. "I mean Rosie mustn't say *done* when she ought to say *did*. I know that Polly Penguin did it. I mean . . ."

"Polly Penguin!" said Rosie, and looked up at her mother as if to say, "You see what I mean? Even Oliver says Polly Penguin did it, so how can you possibly blame me?"

None of this did Rosie any good, and she was sent up to bed with no dinner.

"Don't want beans! Don't want ice cream!" screamed Rosie as she was carried up the stairs. Mom promised Oliver she'd go to school with him the next day and explain about the library book and pay for it so he wouldn't get into trouble.

Polly Penguin was remarkably good for the rest of the evening.

2

Rainbow Dice

The next morning was the day of Oliver's Chess Tournament at school. He was pale and shaky with nerves at breakfast. He couldn't eat his cornflakes because his hand wobbled so much that they all tipped out, and the spoon rattled and chattered against his teeth.

"It's only a game, Oliver," said Dad. "Try and relax and enjoy yourself. That's what it's supposed to be for."

Oliver sat and shook. His skin was as white as if someone had taken all his blood out and filled him up with milk instead.

"But what if I d . . . d . . . don't win?" he said.

"Nobody will think any less of you," said Dad.

"Of course they will," said Oliver. "They'll

think I'm not such a good chess player as some-body else!"

"Does that really matter so very, very much?" said Mom. "Being a brilliant chess player doesn't make you a better person. Most of the famous players I can think of seem to have been either hor-rible or crazy or both. Here, try some toast. You aren't getting anywhere with those cornflakes."

Oliver didn't want any toast. "You just don't understand," he said.

Alice understood. The thing about Oliver was that he could just never bear to lose at anything. It didn't matter if it was chess or tiddlywinks. When we won he gave off a satisfied glow. He was at his nicest. He would even try to help you by telling you where you had gone wrong. But when he lost, a huge black cloud descended over him. The rest of the day would be ruined. He would say: "It's not fair!" or "I had a headache!" or "I wasn't play-ing properly anyway!" or "I couldn't concentrate because my foot was sore!" He had always been the same. He had probably been born that way. Al-ice was very glad she was different. At least she could relax and enjoy games. Oliver never relaxed. He never laughed. He never had any fun.

Of course, this made him very difficult to play games with, and hardly anyone except Rosie would play with him anymore. Mom played chess with him now and then, which was safe enough because Oliver always won. But sometimes Rosie would persuade Oliver to play Rainbow Dice with her, and this was always a dreadful mistake. The trouble with Rainbow Dice was that it was entirely a game of luck. You took three rainbow dice, each with a different color on every face, and then you had to throw the right colors to fill up your board. So being older and smarter didn't help Oliver at all. Rosie was just as likely to win as he was, and to have Rosie beating him at anything made Oliver almost ill.

"I hate this stupid game!" he would shout, knocking the board and all the dice across the carpet. "I hate this family! I want to go and live with Grandma Fox in Bristol!"

Rosie thought this was great fun. "I'm the winner!" she would say happily, collecting all the

dice and putting them neatly back into the box, for all the world as if she were a person who usually picked things up instead of being a person who nearly always threw them onto the floor. "Oliver been naughty. I'm the winner."

It was a strange thing, but Rosie, who had a worse temper than anyone else in the house, and probably a worse temper than anyone in the world, never minded a bit about winning and losing games. Even when Oliver won, she just said, "I'm the winner!"

Oliver tried very hard to explain to her that she had lost. "Look, Rosie," he said. "I just threw a red, which was all I needed. You still need green and yellow. *I'm* the winner."

Now *this* made Rosie angry. It made her so angry that she hurled all the dice, and the shaker and the board, at Oliver. So whoever won, the game ended with dice thrown all around the room and with somebody losing their temper.

Alice never played Rainbow Dice with anyone anymore.

3

You Win Three Bananas

Every Tuesday after school Alice cleaned Aminal's hutch, which was kept out on the patio up against the kitchen wall. She chose Tuesdays because that was the day Oliver went to Chess Club. The good thing about this was that it meant he wasn't there on the patio with Alice, cleaning out Peter's hutch, watching Alice and telling her she wasn't doing it properly.

"You really should clean your guinea pig on Saturdays when I clean Peter Rabbit," he would say. "Then there would be people around to help you." Oliver would never call Aminal by his real name. He said this was because it wasn't a proper name, but the real reason was that he couldn't say it. It simply never came out the right way. He could only say *Animal,* which was quite wrong.

Aminal was what used to come out of Alice's mouth whenever she tried to say *animal,* and Oliver had teased and teased her about it. So when she had been given a guinea pig for her last birthday, she called him Aminal, and all of a sudden her word was right and Oliver's word, *animal,* was wrong.

Alice liked to do things her own way, and she didn't need any help cleaning a hutch out, especially not from Oliver, who never actually helped at all. Rosie trotted outside with her. While Alice was cleaning out Aminal's cage, Rosie would clean out Polly Penguin's. Polly was supposed to live in a shoebox next to Aminal's hutch, but because she was such a particularly naughty penguin, she was very rarely at home.

Alice had a large cardboard box to put Aminal in while she was getting his hutch ready. Sometimes Mom or Dad might let Aminal sit on their lap, but usually they were too busy. On the day of Oliver's Chess Tournament, Dad was home and

Mom was picking Oliver up. Mom was usually the one who picked up Oliver from Chess Club, because she could play chess herself and so she could make some sense of what Oliver was saying about pawns and queens and sacrifices and checkmates. Alice asked Dad if he'd hold Aminal, but he was much too busy making a risotto, which, he said, would be the best risotto they had ever eaten in their lives.

Alice lifted Aminal carefully out of his hutch and lowered him into the box. He shivered and looked up at her sadly, his nose twitching. He had never liked the box. There weren't any windows and he couldn't see anything except sky.

Rosie dropped Polly Penguin into the box with Aminal. Aminal gave Polly Penguin a hopeful sort of sniff. Rosie used Aminal's bedding in Polly Penguin's shoebox, and Polly Penguin was sometimes put in Aminal's hutch to visit. This meant that Polly Penguin was starting to have the same fluffy sawdusty smell as Aminal, and for a few wonderful moments it seemed to Aminal that Polly Penguin might be another guinea pig, come to play.

Alice changed all of Aminal's old smelly bedding, and gave him fresh food and water. Then she went indoors to get a special present she had bought him with fifty cents of her pocket money. It was a sheet of butterfly stickers.

"I want that," said Rosie.

Alice growled at her. She peeled all the stickers off one by one and stuck them carefully to the inside of Aminal's hutch. There were fifteen stickers altogether. By the time she had finished, there were butterflies all over the walls, and two on the ceiling. Alice thought it looked wonderful. She lifted Aminal out of the cardboard box and put him back in his newly decorated hutch. Aminal looked amazed at the sight of the butterflies.

"Polly Penguin wants that," said Rosie dangerously.

"There's all the white pieces left for Polly Penguin," said Alice. "Look." She picked up the sticker page and began to peel off the outside. It all came off in one piece, a rectangle of white sticky paper with butterfly-shaped holes in it. Rosie looked at this for a while, then took it and

began to tear it into pieces, which she stuck on Polly Penguin's shoebox. Alice breathed a sigh of relief.

Suddenly there was the sound of the front door slamming and of Oliver running into the kitchen.

"I won!" he shouted. "I won the Chess Tournament!"

"Wonderful!" said Dad.

"I've got a trophy!" said Oliver.

"Wonderful!" said Dad. "And I've made risotto. It's not as if it were any old risotto. Tender baby button mushrooms, sliced into razor-thin slivers and delicately fried in butter . . ."

Oliver rushed outside to the patio to show Alice and Rosie.

"Look!" he said. "I won!" He was waving something wildly around in the air.

"Can I see?" asked Alice.

Oliver gave her the trophy to look at. It was really very interesting. It was shaped like a silver goblet, but with handles on both sides, and where the handles joined the cup the silver had been made into the shape of a chess king and queen. The trophy had a wooden base, which had a pattern on top of pale and dark brown squares like a chess board. Alice couldn't imagine ever being smart enough to win such a glorious thing. For a moment she felt quite proud to have Oliver for a brother. This wasn't something she felt very often.

Rosie looked at the trophy and at Oliver. "Don't want that stupid shiny cup!" she shouted, before Oliver had a chance to tell her she couldn't have it.

Mom came out to join them on the patio. "What's all this about?" she said. "A trophy! I think this deserves a treat, Oliver. Though for heaven's sake don't ask for chicken legs for dinner, because your father's cooking risotto and we all have to pretend it's the best risotto there's ever been in the world."

"I heard that!" shouted Dad from inside.

"All I want is to play chess!" said Oliver. "I can't think of anything else but chess. Let's play a game, Mom."

"But you always win!" said Mom.

This was not a problem for Oliver.

"All right then," said Mom. "Let me just say hello to Animal, I mean . . ."

She drew a deep breath, *"Aminal."*

"Well done," said Alice. Mom bent down and peered into the hutch.

"Goodness!" she said. "He's had the decorators over!"

"What do you mean?" said Oliver, crouching down beside her.

"Butterflies!" said Mom. Aminal was huddled in the far corner of his hutch, still blinking with astonishment.

"Do you think he likes them?" Alice asked nervously. For all she knew, guinea pigs were terrified of butterflies and Aminal would have nightmares for weeks.

"He doesn't look as if he does," said Oliver.

"Oh, I think he will," said Mom. "I think he'll be glad for something to look at, once he gets used to them. I remember when we had the front room decorated it took your father months to get used to it, and he's fine now. I wouldn't worry."

Alice went indoors with them to watch the chess game. It always sounded as if it ought to be interesting — more interesting than anything else that was going on in the house, anyway. Then after a few minutes she would remember what it was really like. Alice enjoyed most games, but chess was absolutely no fun at all. Mom and Oliver just sat there and stared at the board, which was just plain brown and white squares. None of them said "Go back one square" or "Advance to Go" or "Collect a thousand dollars" or anything like that. There weren't any dice to roll or cards to pick up with exciting messages like "You win three bananas from the player on your left."

And then there was Oliver himself. He sat hunched tight, his fists clenched white, all of him screwed up into a ball of concentration. He was trying so hard he was nearly bursting. It seemed a great waste of effort because he always seemed to win quite easily. There was something about the sight of Oliver playing chess that made Alice want to rush up and down the yard, waving her arms about like a windmill and shouting complete nonsense at the top of her voice.

She couldn't imagine what would happen if Oliver lost at anything. But, of course, he never did.

4

Pavement Narrows Quarter-mile Ahead

The weekend after that was Grandma Fox's birthday. Every year they all drove down to Bristol for the day with her birthday present. Last year Rosie had drawn scribbles all over Grandma Fox's nice white hall with a sticky red felt pen. Alice had hoped that this meant that they wouldn't have to go again, but it seemed that Rosie had been forgiven.

Of course Grandpa Fox would be there as well, but you never really thought of it as visiting him because he never seemed to be around. He was always busy decorating something or fixing something or building something or doing secret things in the shed. He would poke his head through the door and say hello, and he hoped

they wouldn't mind if he didn't stop, because he was right in the middle of his grouting and the plaster would set. He seemed to spend more time in the shed than he did in the house. Alice thought this was very sensible of him. If she had to live with Grandma Fox all the time, she'd want to move out to the shed as well.

When Grandpa Fox had seen what Rosie had done to the hall with the red pen, he had been quite excited about it. "I'll have to redecorate this from top to bottom now!" he said. He looked like someone who had just been given a present. Grandpa Fox had a soft spot for Rosie, and often took her off to help him in the garden.

Grandma Fox did *not* have a soft spot for Rosie. Grandma Fox liked Oliver best. She thought Oliver was absolutely wonderful. She thought Oliver was exactly what children ought to be like. She had twice as many photographs of Oliver as she did of Alice or Rosie, and she always gave him much better presents. She didn't mind Alice, as long as Alice was quiet and good and didn't annoy her, but then she never took much notice of her, either. Rosie, Grandma thought, was the worst child in the world.

The Singers had to leave early Saturday morning.

"Are you sure Aminal will be all right?" Alice asked for the hundredth time, as Mom and Dad loaded bags into the trunk. It would be a long lonely day for Aminal, and she was sure he'd miss her, and if he got sick there would be nobody to look after him.

"Don't worry," said Dad. "You've filled up his water bottle and given him plenty of food. He'll be just fine. He's got Peter Rabbit for company!"

Alice didn't think much of that. Oliver's rabbit was the most boring animal she had ever known in her life. He was getting more and more like Oliver all the time. She could just imagine what it would be like for poor Aminal, with Peter Rabbit sitting there in the hutch opposite gazing over at him in a sniffy sort of way, as if to say that Aminal was making a mess with his food and he really ought to learn to eat properly. Polly Penguin would be better company, only Polly Penguin had mysteriously disappeared a couple of days ago. But there was nothing more Alice could do for Aminal, so she got into the car.

Alice always had to sit in the middle of the back seat, the very worst place. This was because Rosie's car seat had to go next to one window, and Oliver had to sit by the other one because otherwise he got carsick. Alice had never seen Oliver get carsick, but he said this was because he always sat by the window.

Rosie could open the belt and straps of her car seat, so she had to be tied in with string. "I want Polly Penguin!" she cried, while Mom tied several very tight knots.

"Absolutely not," said Mom. It had been decided that Polly Penguin was too naughty to be allowed to go to Grandma Fox's. There was no telling what might happen if Polly Penguin was let loose on Grandma's beautiful, perfectly tidy house.

Alice slid into her place, Oliver climbed in beside her, and Mom got into the driver's seat. Mom and Dad usually did half the driving each,

stopping halfway to untie Rosie and take her to the bathroom.

"Let's play the Alphabet Game!" said Oliver to Alice.

"All right," said Alice. She liked the Alphabet Game. What you had to do was to look out of the window and find a word starting with A, then one with B, then one with C, all the way through to Z. Alice had never in her life got to Z. She usually got stuck on Q and then fell asleep somewhere on the highway. It was a safe game to play because Oliver always won. As Oliver was at least nine inches taller than Alice and he had a window to look out of while she was stuck in the middle, this wasn't surprising.

They both always got A very quickly because their road was called Ashton Road and the road at the end of it was called South Avenue. After that it depended which way they were going. If they were heading towards the highway, you had to try very hard to get as far in the alphabet as you could before the highway began, because after that there were no street names or stores and it got very difficult. There was nothing but road signs and trucks on the highway, and Oliver nearly always saw those first.

Alice was on E and Oliver was on G when Rosie suddenly said: "Polly Penguin did hide in the car!"

There was a long silence.

"Where did Polly Penguin hide, Rosie?" asked Dad.

"Under your seat," said Rosie, shaking her head sadly at the wickedness of Polly Penguin.

Alice bent down, scrabbled around under Dad's car seat and pulled Polly out.

"Very naughty!" said Rosie sorrowfully.

"G!" said Oliver. "Gordon's Pharmacy."

"Rosie," said Mom, "if Polly Penguin does one single naughty thing at Grandma Fox's, just one, she's going in the trash!"

Alice thought this was a bit much. "Polly Penguin used to be mine!" she said. "You can't do that!"

"In the trash," said Mom. Alice sighed. It was hard enough to keep out of trouble herself, and now shc'd havc to keep an eye on Rosie as well.

"H!" said Oliver. "Halifax Building Society."

Alice had to work very hard to catch up now. Luckily Oliver got stuck on K for quite a long time, and when they reached the highway she was on P and he was on Q.

They drove on for quite a long time without anyone getting anything, and Mom and Dad began to talk about changing the rules for the really difficult letters like Q and X and Z.

"The game just gets stuck on Q every time," said Mom. "Perhaps we should let them count if they see it on a car license plate."

"That would be too easy," said Dad.

"Or perhaps it should count if you see a word with a Q in it anywhere."

"You're too soft," said Dad.

"X!" said Rosic.

"Don't be silly, Rosie," said Oliver. "You haven't even got an A yet."

"X!" said Rosie, cuddling Polly Penguin. "I got an X!"

Oliver, who had had his nose pressed up against his window watching the trucks go by in the other direction, turned around and started to explain to Rosie why she couldn't have an X. "If you're going to play, then you must play properly, Rosie. Now, what you do is . . ."

Alice yawned. She couldn't understand why Oliver didn't just ignore Rosie. She thought she might be about to fall asleep. She hadn't even got P yet, let alone Q. And then, suddenly, a large blue sign came into view through the front window. Oliver, who was still telling Rosie the rules, hadn't seen it. And the sign grew close enough for Alice to read it. She blinked. She could hardly believe it. The sign said:

> **PAVEMENT NARROWS**
> **QUARTER-MILE**
> **AHEAD**

"P and Q!" yelled Alice. "Pavement Narrows Quarter-mile Ahead!"

"Well done, Alice!" said Dad.

"What?" screamed Oliver, looking around just in time to see the sign disappear behind them in a flash. "What did she say?"

"Pavement Narrows Quarter-mile Ahead!" sang Alice. She had gotten Q! For the first time in her life she had gotten Q, and she was beating Oliver!

"It couldn't have been!" said Oliver. "There's no such sign! I've never seen one before! You didn't see it, did you, Dad?"

"I'm afraid I did," said Dad.

"But it's not fair!" shouted Oliver. "I wasn't looking because I had to tell Rosie how to play properly. One of you should have told her!"

"I didn't really think it mattered," said Mom. "Calm down, Oliver. If you scream into my ear like that again I'll have an accident."

"But it's not *fair*," moaned Oliver. "I would have seen it first!"

"W!" said Rosie, with a wicked glint in her

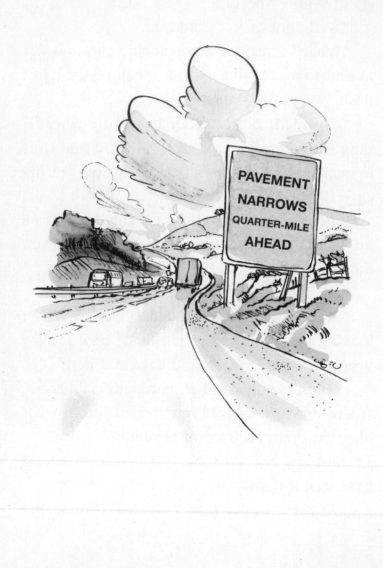

eye. Oliver screwed up his fists and pressed them up against his eyes and went very quiet. And so he didn't see what Alice could see: an enormous, slow, green truck up ahead in the distance. They were catching up to it fast. Alice squeezed a sideways glance at Oliver out of the corner of her eye. He still wasn't looking. And Alice could see that there were several words on the back of the truck. Whatever they were, if they were any use at all, Alice would get them.

And then they were close enough to read the words. It couldn't be true, could it? Could it? Could it possibly? She checked and double-checked. She triple-checked. It was true. This was what it said on the back of the truck:

**LONG VEHICLE
ROUTINE SKID
TESTING UNDER
WAY**

"R, S, T, U, V, and W!" said Alice.

Mom and Dad both cheered.

"I think that's the world record!" said Mom. "I've never seen anything like it!"

"That definitely wins a prize!" said Dad.

From Alice's right there came a loud noise. It was the sound of Oliver bursting into tears.

The rest of the trip was no fun at all.

5

Grandma and Grandpa Fox

Twenty minutes later, when they stopped at a gas station to untie Rosie and change drivers, Oliver refused to get out of the car. He wouldn't talk to anybody. He just sat scrunched up in the corner of the back seat and didn't move.

"Come along, old man," said Dad.

Oliver buried his head in his hands and made a sniffling noise.

"Move!" said Dad. "Out!"

Nothing happened.

"I'll wet my pants," said Rosie, wriggling and squirming.

"All right, then, we'll leave you here," said Dad to Oliver.

Mom sighed. "We can't really leave him on his

35

own," she said. "I'll stay and talk to him. Alice, you go with your father and take Rosie to the bathroom."

Alice groaned. Taking Rosie to a public bathroom was a nightmare. These were just some of the things Rosie had done so far in public bathrooms:

1. Dropped her new furry mittens into the toilet.
2. Used a whole roll of toilet paper, which caused a very nasty flood.
3. Stolen a purse from the woman in the next stall by pulling it under the wall by the strap. The police were very understanding, but Alice had nearly died of shame.

So you had to go in with her and watch her with eyes in the back of your head, and there was never enough room, and Rosie would stick her legs straight out in front and kick you in the stomach. And then she would insist on flushing the toilet herself, even if you had to lift her up to reach it. And then you had to lift her up to reach the sink so that she could wash her hands, and you didn't have a free hand to turn the faucet on for her, and you never knew how the faucets were going to work anyway, and there would always be a horrible mess with the soap. And everyone else would be *watching* you. And then you would have to stand around waiting for the automatic hand dryer to turn itself off, because Rosie would never leave until it had finished. Her arms weren't long enough to reach that either, so she always ended up dripping wet anyway, and you had to hold her hand to get her out, so you ended up damp yourself.

"Sorry about that, Alice," said Dad, as Alice and Rosie came out from the women's bathroom, Alice holding on grimly, Rosie struggling to escape.

"That was *terrible*," said Alice. She could have *killed* Oliver. They should have *made* him get out of the car.

"Let's go to the store here and find something for your prize," said Dad, grabbing Rosie and lifting her up onto his shoulders.

Alice cheered up at that. She had almost forgotten about the prize. It didn't seem real, somehow. She still could hardly believe that she had

actually beaten Oliver at anything, let alone broken the Alphabet Game world record. She wandered around in a daze. There were puzzles and crayons and magazines and books and candy, but while she would have *quite* liked any of these things, there was nothing that seemed special enough for this prize. She explained this to Dad and he understood perfectly.

"We'll save it for when you see something special enough," he said.

"You won't forget, will you?" It might take weeks before something special turned up. It might take *months*.

"I'll give you a written promise," said Dad. He took some paper and a pen from his pocket, wrote something down, tore it off, and gave it to Alice. It said: "I owe Alice one special thing for breaking the world record at the Alphabet Game."

This seemed perfect to Alice.

But back in the car things hadn't improved at all.

"Oliver wasn't in the mood for talking," said Mom. "I gave up trying after a while."

39

"I'm sure he'll cheer up when we get to Grandma Fox's," said Dad, climbing into the driver's seat. "He always does."

Oliver sniffed. Dad started the car and pulled out of the gas station back onto the highway.

Just before they got to Grandma Fox's house they drove past something exciting. There were brightly colored vans and trucks parked in a field, and all around were carousels, stalls, and swingboat rides, with a huge ferris wheel in the middle circling up into the sky. A fairground!

"Look!" squeaked Alice. "The fair! Can we go? Please?"

"Sorry, Alice," said Mom. "We're only here for the day, and we're visiting Grandma Fox for her birthday."

Alice sighed. Grandma Fox never seemed to like Alice particularly, so you'd think she'd be glad for Alice to be at the fair and out of her way. All of a sudden a vivid memory came into her head. "That fair was here last year too!" she said. "And we couldn't go then either!"

"It comes here every autumn," said Mom.

"And we told Grandma Fox about it," said Alice, still remembering, "and she said it was dirty and rough."

"I'm afraid so," said Dad. They drove on past the fair, and Alice turned to gaze out of the back window as it disappeared. It wasn't open yet, but she could almost see the flashing lights of the carousels as they whirled round, and hear the loud distorted magical sound of the fairground music. It made it seem a hundred times worse that they were going to Grandma Fox's.

A few minutes later they had arrived, and Dad parked the car in the road. Mom untied Rosie, who was cuddling Polly Penguin and smiling like a little angel, and they all piled out and went to ring the doorbell.

Except for Oliver. Oliver stayed in the car, all cold and pale, with his arms folded tight. He hadn't spoken to anyone for an hour and a half and he didn't move.

Grandma Fox opened the door and looked at them. "Hello, everyone!" she said. She gave Mom a kiss and smiled all around, the smile only fading as she caught sight of Rosie, who stood still and sweet and beamed up at her warmly.

"Hello, Grandma!" said Rosie.

"Hello, Roseanna," said Grandma faintly. Grandma Fox was the only person in the world who called Rosie by her full name. She gazed down at Rosie as if wishing to check her for weapons before allowing her in the house. Rosie snuggled up against Mom's legs and fluttered her eyelashes and pretended to be shy. Grandma Fox looked more suspicious at this than if Rosie had charged at her full-tilt waving a thick red felt pen.

Then Grandma said, "Where's Oliver?"

"In the car," said Dad.

Now he's going to get it, thought Alice. Suddenly it seemed that this was the moment she'd been waiting for all her life. At last Grandma Fox, who thought that Oliver was perfect and had never seen what he could *really* be like, was going to see him being sulky and rude. Really, really rude. Ruder than Alice had ever been in her life. And all because he'd lost a game and Alice was World Champion. Alice lost games all the time, and it seemed that she had been losing games to Oliver ever since she had been born. And she had never ever minded or complained or sulked. Alice had never been naughty like Rosie. She had always been good and quiet and polite and behaved properly, and all these years Grandma Fox had preferred Oliver anyway. Well, all that was about to change. Because Grandma Fox got absolutely *furious* about rudeness. Surely nothing would ever be the same again.

But —

"Oh, he hasn't been carsick, has he?" said Grandma. "Poor Oliver. Alice, I hope you didn't have a silly little fight over the window seat, did you? You know Oliver feels *so* poorly if he can't sit by a window." And before Alice could say a word, Grandma Fox had swept out to their car and opened Oliver's door and was giving him a big hug.

Oliver got out of the car. He staggered out, holding his tummy. He looked so pale and ill that anyone would think he *had* been carsick.

"Come in and sit quietly and have a nice cool

drink," said Grandma. And that was the end of that.

Alice couldn't believe it. Dad gave her shoulder a big squeeze, as if to say he knew what she was feeling. He pointed to her pocket, where she had hidden her secret note from him. Alice gave a faint smile. But the day had fallen to pieces. For a moment she wished that the Special Thing that Dad owed her could be that they never had to drive to Bristol and see Grandma Fox again. But she knew this would never happen because she was their grandma and they would always have to see her, forever.

Inside, Oliver had had a drink of old-fashioned lemonade and thought he was starting to feel a bit better. Although he still didn't feel completely well, he managed to be brave enough to go out to the car and get Grandma's birthday present, a large plant in a terra-cotta pot which they'd had to wedge in with cushions in the trunk so it wouldn't fall over.

"Oh, thank you, Oliver!" said Grandma. "Thank you, everybody!" she remembered to say a moment afterwards. Grandpa Fox poked his head in through the back door and said hello to everybody, and he hoped they'd excuse him if he didn't come in, but he was turning over the vegetable garden and his boots were squelchy with mud from tip to toe.

Grandma put her plant on the porch and made toasted sandwiches for lunch. Alice sat quiet and still in a corner and wondered what on earth they were going to do for the rest of the day. Grandpa took his muddy boots off and puttered inside for a sandwich. This reminded Oliver to get out his chess trophy to show everyone.

"Clever boy," said Grandpa, from underneath Rosie, who had climbed on his knee with Polly Penguin and was feeding him bits of toasted sandwich.

Grandma took the trophy in her hands and turned it around and around. You would think she had never seen a trophy in her life before. She looked at it and then looked at Oliver and back at the trophy again as if she were about to burst. Oliver managed to force down three toasted sandwiches despite having been feeling so poorly. Alice looked at the clock and worked out that there were at least six hours left before they could start driving back and possibly even seven. And then there would be two and a half hours in the car, and she'd have to go straight to bed when they got back, and that would be *it*.

Somehow she had expected more of a day when she had broken a world record. Somehow Oliver had managed to spoil it and he had gotten away with it.

6

Top of the World

Things got worse. After lunch Grandpa put Rosie's pink elephant boots on and took her and Polly Penguin back outside to do gardening. Dad went out with them to look at the vegetables. He was always meaning to grow vegetables himself. But somehow everything Grandpa Fox planted grew and grew, while everything Dad planted shrivelled up and died or got eaten by slugs.

"They have the happiest, fattest slugs back home," Dad said. "All the slugs in the neighborhood come to the Singer house for parties. I might as well give up and put out cookies and balloons for the slugs so they can really enjoy themselves. I might as well put out cans of soda for them to wash the lettuce down. It's hopeless."

Alice gazed bleakly out through the window at them. "And now let me tell you what I've got planned for this afternoon," Grandma Fox was saying. "I know a very special store in town where they sell chess sets. I know you've only got an old cheap one, and I thought it was time Oliver had a really nice set of his own. So I thought we'd all go downtown and Oliver can choose a set, as a special treat for winning his school Chess Tournament."

"Now that's a wonderful idea," said Mom, brightening up. Mom *loved* going shopping. "As it happens, I need some new shoes. There must be at least half a dozen shoe shops to choose from."

A huge gloomy blackness fell on Alice at the thought of being carted around to six different stores while Mom tried on shoes.

"And I need a blouse!" said Grandma. "Good. We'll leave in a half hour, then. Roseanna seems quite happy in the garden, so I think we'll leave her behind. That will mean we can do our shopping in peace. Good."

This was absolutely desperate. Shoes! Blouses! Chess sets! Without Rosie screaming and whining that she wanted to go home it could take *hours*. And it was a Saturday afternoon, and there would be millions of people pushing and shoving and trampling on Alice and knocking her over. Her mother never seemed to notice this.

Suddenly Alice had an idea. She raced out of the room and into the back yard.

"Dad!" she shouted.

Dad came over. "What's the matter?"

"Shopping!" said Alice.

"Shopping?" said Dad.

"Grandma wants us all to go shopping for a chess set downtown!" said Alice.

"Oh dear," said Dad.

"And they're going to buy shoes and blouses!" said Alice.

"Not shoes and blouses!" said Dad, looking worried.

"They'll probably go to Spencers," said Alice. "Dad, I've known Mom spend a whole hour in the women's section of Spencers!"

"It's not possible!" said Dad, looking seriously alarmed.

"A whole hour!" said Alice. "And that's before she even *starts* on the shoe stores. You don't know what it's like. You never go. I've *been*."

"Alice," said Dad, "this is desperate."

"That's what I thought," said Alice.

"We have to make a plan," said Dad.

"I've got a plan!" said Alice.

"You do?" said Dad.

"We'll go to the fair!" said Alice.

"We'll go to the fair!" said Dad. "Hang on a second. *What* did you just say?"

"I said, we'll go to the fair!" said Alice. She pulled out the secret note from her pocket and read it out loud. "'I owe Alice one special thing for breaking the world record at the Alphabet Game.' This is the special thing I want."

"Hmm," said Dad. "I don't know about that. I mean . . ."

"Shoe shopping!" said Alice.

"But what about Rosie and Oliver?" said Dad, shuddering at the very thought of shoe shops.

"Rosie's quite happy here with Grandpa," said Alice, pointing. "Look." Dad looked. It was true. Rosie was standing ankle deep in mud, digging with a little spade and chattering to Grandpa Fox. From time to time Grandpa said, "Polly Penguin did *what?*" They looked completely peaceful together.

"And Oliver has to choose his chess set," said Alice. The thought that Oliver would also have to spend hours looking at blouses in Marks and Spencers didn't bother her one little bit. He deserved it for being such a bad loser at the Alphabet Game. He deserved it for making Mom stay with him so Alice had to take Rosie to the bathroom. He . . . he just *deserved* it.

So Dad agreed that they would go to the fair. Grandma Fox was horrified when they told her. "But it's dirty and rough!" she said.

"Never mind," said Dad, putting his arm around Alice. "I'll take good care of both of us."

Alice could see a silent scream starting to explode inside Oliver. He hated going shopping as much as she did. He was *dying* to go to the fair. But he couldn't say a word, because then Grandma Fox would be offended and he wouldn't get his chess set.

Things were working out rather well.

The fair was magic. Dad said they could stay as long as it took them to spend twenty dollars, which Alice thought would last forever, but which actually disappeared in about an hour.

They went on the ghost train, which wasn't even a bit scary, and on the Octopus, which was brilliant. They rode on the swingboats and the flying teacups, and Alice won two baby trolls by rolling balls into slots with numbers and making them add up to twenty-one. She let Dad have a turn at rifle shooting and he won another baby troll. But the best thing was the ferris wheel. At first she hadn't thought she'd get her father to go on it.

"I'm scared!" he said. "I want a hot dog!"

Alice counted the money that was left, and said he could have a hot dog, but only if he went on the ferris wheel with her.

"You're very cruel," said Dad.

"You can have a hot dog with onions!" said Alice.

"I'll have to have ketchup and mustard as well if I'm going on that thing," said Dad, gazing up into the sky with a horrified expression on his face. "It might be the last meal I ever eat!"

"We better go on the ferris wheel first in case you're sick," said Alice, and they got in line. A couple of minutes later the wheel stopped and the fairground man began to load people on. When it was their turn, he sat them down in a swingy seat and snapped a metal bar shut to hold them in.

"I want to go home!" squeaked Dad.

The fairground man winked and pulled a lever, and suddenly the wheel began to turn, carrying them up, up, up to the very top. They sat there, swinging gently, while more people got on at the bottom. Alice could see all of Bristol over the tops of the trees. She was so excited she couldn't speak. She could hardly breathe. And then the ride started, and the wheel spun round and round, round and round, with the lights

flashing and the music blaring out, and Alice wasn't stuck on the ground watching, she was in it, part of it, and she could see everything in the world.

"I can see London!" she screamed. Everyone was screaming. "I can see Scotland, I can see Australia, I can see the moon!" She was on top of the world and she had broken a world record. It was her day, after all.

7

Recently Buried Chickens

They spent the last of the money on two hot dogs and wandered back to the car with the baby trolls. Alice was so happy she was half afraid she was dreaming, and in a moment she'd wake up to find herself at the back of a long, bad-tempered line at the department store. She decided to give one troll each to Oliver and Rosie because they hadn't been to the fair.

When they got back everyone was watching television while dinner cooked in the oven. Oliver looked half asleep, which wasn't surprising, because going shopping on a Saturday was just about the most tiring thing Alice could think of. Rosie and Polly Penguin were perched on Grandpa Fox's knee as usual.

And Mom was surrounded by the most enormous pile of shopping bags. She had bought a sweater for Alice and a dress for Rosie and socks and a shirt for Oliver, and three pairs of shoes for herself. She had bought a set of pillowcases and two cushion covers, three paperback books and a CD, and a pair of black tights with sparkles. She had bought a bath sponge shaped like a pineapple and a nail brush shaped like a melon. They must have had to stand in a dozen different lines.

"What, no soap shaped like a strawberry?" said Dad. "No quilted comforter? No Second World War air raid shelter? How are we ever going to manage?"

Mom opened the last bag and pulled out a box of Dad's favorite chocolates.

"Now you're talking!" said Dad, tearing at the wrapping.

"We're just about to have dinner!" said Grandma. Dad put the chocolates down in a hurry.

Mom came over and gave Alice a hug. "You're looking tired," she said.

Alice didn't feel one bit tired, just dazed, but

she wasn't going to say so because being tired was a thing that might make Mom and Dad decide to go home earlier.

"Never mind," said Mom. "After dinner Grandma wants to have one quick game of chess with Oliver, and then we'll set off and you can have a nice nap in the car."

"I didn't know Grandma could play chess!" said Alice.

"Of course she can," said Mom. "Who do you think taught me?"

They had chicken casserole and fresh fruit salad for dinner, and then it was time for the chess game. Alice hoped Oliver wouldn't take too long to win. It was half past six already.

"Oliver, you can put your baby troll on the table to be your lucky mascot if you like," Alice said. She had seen people do this on television. Once she had seen someone bring along a cabbage to be their lucky mascot, and the quizmaster had smiled politely at the cabbage and said hello to it. Perhaps the troll would help Oliver to win more quickly, and then they could go home.

"Thank you, Alice," said Oliver, who was looking a bit livelier since he'd had his dinner. He perched the baby troll on the table next to his new chess board, which was beautiful. The old set had cheap little plastic pieces and a flimsy board, which folded down the middle and was all cracked and torn along the fold. *This* chess board was made of solid wood, and so were the pieces. It was a very fine chess set. If only you could do something interesting with it, like rolling balls at it and seeing how many pieces you could knock over! But chess wasn't like that at all. Oliver frowned, leaned forward, and moved a white piece. The game had begun.

Alice watched for the first few minutes. Grandma Fox moved her black pieces quickly and calmly. She didn't look one bit worried about playing against Oliver. Alice remembered that Grandma Fox wasn't the sort of Grandma who stayed at home all day looking after the house, like Alice's other Grandma. Grandma Fox was a schoolteacher. She taught chemistry. She was probably quite clever.

Oliver was leaning further and further forward, his fists screwed up into clenched white balls and his knuckles digging into the sides of his head. His lips were tight and thin and his forehead one big frown. Alice had seen all this before. She looked around, and suddenly noticed that Rosie and Polly Penguin had disappeared. How long had they been gone? They could be anywhere. They could be doing anything. And if they'd done something bad, Mom was going to throw Polly Penguin in the trash, and then Rosie would throw a tantrum. This was an emergency!

But Rosie and Polly Penguin were sitting halfway up the stairs, looking good as gold. In fact, Rosie had that especially good look that came over her when she had just emptied herself of badness by doing something really, really wicked.

"Rosie," said Alice, "tell me what you've done. Quickly!" There might still be time to go and clean it up, while everyone was busy watching the chess game.

"Polly Penguin been good!" said Rosie.

Alice gave Rosie a long hard look.

"Are you *sure?*" she said.

"Good!" said Rosie, gazing up at Alice with huge brown innocent eyes. Alice sighed. She would have to check the whole house. She took Rosie and Polly Penguin with her, to keep an eye on them.

Alice, Rosie, and Polly Penguin tiptoed in and out of every room in Grandma Fox's house while Alice checked for signs of mischief. They looked everywhere. Alice peered inside the toilet in search of furry mittens, and crouched down to look under Grandma's bed. She turned all Grandma's shoes upside down and shook them. She opened the oven and the washing machine and inspected the insides. She even poked her head around the back door to examine the garden for evidence of recently buried chickens.

There was nothing. Everything was as it should be.

"Polly Penguin been good!" said Rosie again. Rosie had been following Alice around, her eyes huge with delight. Rosie thought it was a great joke. Alice didn't know what to make of it. Rosie

63

had been perfectly good all day. Perhaps she had decided to have good days. This wasn't necessarily such a wonderful thing. If you *knew* she had been naughty, then you had to keep looking until you'd found what she'd done, but at least once you'd found it you could relax. If she *might* have been good, you didn't know if you could stop looking or not.

It seemed that life only ever got more and more complicated.

8

Checkmate

Alice took Rosie's hand and they went back in to see if the chess game had finished. Right away she could see that something was wrong. The room was full of the most silent silence she had ever heard. Oliver was slumped forward, his hands covering his face. The bits of face that showed between his fingers were a dead gray color. And, on the chess board, there were more black pieces than white. Alice counted, and counted again. Grandma Fox had eight pieces and Oliver only had six.

Oliver was going to lose.

Grandma moved a black knight and said, "Check." This was usually what Oliver said, just before he won. When he won, he said, "Checkmate."

Oliver moved his white king.

Grandma moved a black bishop. "Check."

Oliver banged his hand hard on the table. Mom and Dad looked at each other. Oliver moved his white king.

Grandma moved the black knight again and said, "Checkmate."

For a moment the world stood still.

Then something terrible happened. All the frustrations of the day began to boil up inside Oliver like a fire of anger and misery. Losing the Alphabet Game to Alice and Alice getting the world record. Having to shop with Mom and Grandma while Alice went to the fair. And now losing a game of chess to Grandma Fox with his entire family watching. Something in Oliver exploded.

"It's not fair!" he screamed, picking up the chess board and all the pieces and hurling them onto the floor. "I hate you all!" Nothing was left on the table except the baby troll. Oliver grabbed it and threw it at Alice. "You and your stupid lucky trolls!" he shouted. "It made me lose! I never had a troll before and I never lost! It's all your fault!"

Alice managed to catch the troll. And then the room froze. Nobody moved. Nobody said a word. And the most dreadful silence of all was that of Grandma Fox. She gazed at Oliver as if she didn't recognize him. As if she had never really known him before.

Rosie was the first to move. She slipped down off Grandpa Fox's knee, from where she had been watching with her mouth wide open with astonishment, and started picking up the chess pieces. "Oliver been naughty!" she said, putting all the pieces back in their beautiful new wooden box. "Oliver been naughty. Grandma is the winner!"

And then Grandma rose to her feet.

"Thank you, Roseanna," she said. To Alice's amazement, she reached down and picked Rosie up. "You have been a very good child today. I'm glad to see that you're growing up." Rosie gazed proudly around the room as if to say, "Well, look at this!"

And then Grandma Fox turned to Oliver.

"I have never seen such disgraceful behavior in my life," she said. "You clearly aren't old enough to have such a thing as a proper chess set. I have changed my mind. I will keep it here and use it myself."

"No!" cried Oliver, and burst into floods of tears.

"I'm afraid so," said Grandma. She took the chess board and pieces and shut them up firmly in a cupboard. "And you're to apologize to Alice."

This was more than Oliver could bear and he ran out of the room.

"Oh, Oliver . . ." said Mom, and hurried off after him.

Alice sat quietly in the corner holding Oliver's troll. She felt all mixed up. She *had* wanted something bad to happen to Oliver, and it had. He had to go shopping instead of going to the fair. And that should have been it. But now even worse things were happening to him, and Alice had had enough. This was *too much*. She wasn't enjoying it at all. From the hall came the sounds of Oliver crying and Mom making soothing noises.

"Well," said Dad. "I think we'd better be going home."

The trip back was even worse than the trip there, because Oliver kept making little sniffy sobbing noises and nobody could make him stop until just after Reading, when, at last, he fell asleep. Rosie had already been sleeping for an hour. Alice sat in the dark as they sped along the highway, trying to make sense of the day. Everyone had been the opposite of what they were usually. Rosie had been good. Oliver had been very bad. And Alice, who never won anything, had become a world champion. It was all very strange.

She looked down at her lap and the two baby trolls, hers and the one that had been Oliver's. She didn't know what to do with this troll now. Somehow she didn't really want it for herself. She turned around and put the troll at the back of the car with the road maps, where it could enjoy the view through the back window. She was still wondering what to do with it when she fell asleep.

9

P-Q

Rosie's troll, who was named Molly, went to live outside in Polly Penguin's shoebox, and drowned in a thunderstorm a few weeks later.

Alice's troll, who was named Hideous, moved into the hutch with Aminal and the butterflies. Alice was secretly thinking of changing Aminal's name. Now that everyone in the family could say both *Aminal* and *Animal* (except for Oliver, who always called Aminal "your guinea pig"), there didn't seem any point to it any more, and she thought she might call him Alexander instead.

Polly Penguin continued to be almost completely good. But then at Christmas Grandma Fox gave Rosie an adorable cuddly owl called Ollie. Ollie Owl was by far the nicest present she had ever bought Rosie, but you only had to look into Ollie's eyes to know that she was not going to be a well-behaved sort of owl. There followed a most unfortunate accident involving the Christmas turkey, a tube of glue, a bottle of family-size baby shampoo, a packet of instant oatmeal, and the microwave oven. Rosie, Polly, and Ollie were all sent up to their rooms while everyone else tried to scrape the mess off the walls, but Christmas dinner was ruined and in the end they had to have frozen pizza.

Oliver was never quite the same again after the visit to Grandma Fox. For the next three days after the Worst Day of His Life, he hid away in his room. He barely spoke a word and he hardly ate a thing. When he eventually came out, he seemed to have grown three inches taller. He wrote a long letter to Grandma Fox, and received a letter in return. Nobody ever knew what the letters said except for Grandma and Oliver. When they next went down to visit, just before Christmas, Grandma gave Oliver a hug as usual. But this time she gave almost exactly the same hugs to

Alice and to Rosie. You could hardly tell the difference anymore.

And, after lunch, to Alice's horror, Grandma and Oliver played chess again. This time nobody wanted to watch. Grandpa and Rosie were busy tiling the bathroom. Dad was dozing in front of the television. And Mom was going into Bristol to do some last-minute Christmas shopping.

"I'll come with you!" said Alice.

"Shopping?" said Mom in amazement.

"Anything!" said Alice. Anything to get out of the house.

When they got back, with a total of eight bags, Alice tiptoed inside very warily. But there were Oliver and Grandma, sitting on the sofa and talking quietly to each other.

"How did it go?" asked Mom.

"Oliver lost," said Grandma. "But he lost gracefully this time, and he played a better game than before. One day he'll be beating me. But not for another five years!"

Oliver smiled sheepishly. And Grandma Fox let him have the beautiful chess set back, as his

Christmas present. Rosie got Ollie Owl. And for Alice, there was a clay modeling set, which you could use to make animals and jewelry and bake it hard in the oven.

It was a much better visit than the last one.

Oliver never played the Alphabet Game again. Alice asked him to play on the way down to Bristol, but he explained that he was feeling too carsick. She asked him to play on the way back, but he couldn't manage because his legs were aching so much.

And the troll that would have been Oliver's? She somehow stayed on the back of the car and became the Car Troll. She was named P-Q.

"P-Q?" said Dad, when he heard. "Strange sort of name, isn't it?"

"It's because she's a well-behaved troll and always minds her p's and q's," said Alice, looking sideways at Oliver, who pretended not to hear. But this was not the real reason. Alice knew the real reason, and Oliver knew the real reason. The real reason was the sign that said:

Pavement Narrows
Quarter-mile
Ahead

It was still there on the highway and every time they passed it, Alice would turn around, reach P-Q down from the back window, and wave the troll's fat little arm gently at the sign. She would never forget the day she broke the world record. And, for sure, neither would Oliver.